Rainbow and the Unicorn

Written by SJ Dawson
Illustrated by Jayne Farrer

Artwork
All illustrations created by Jayne Farrer:

www.jaynefarrer.com

Printed in the United Kingdom
First Printing, 2021
ISBN: Print (Soft Cover): 978-1-912677-16-0

Published by Purple Parrot Publishing
www.purpleparrotpublishing.co.uk

About this book

If you have read the first two books in the *Rainbow Dust* series, you will be aware that the second book was older and more developed than the first book.

I have continued in this vein, so that the stories and my main characters grow with my readers. I feel quite strongly that there appears to be a gap between picture books and chapter book, so this book is between the two. It is for slightly older readers, is longer and has a more in-depth story but still has some illustrations.

I hope you all enjoy reading *Rainbow Dust and the Dueno*.

Look out for the fourth and final adventure.

Noticing the hands on her watch spinning round and round, Jessica rushes to her bedroom window. A rainbow swoops across the sky, landing on the grass.

"Oh no," she shouts, rushing down the stairs and out of her grandmother's white stone cottage.

She runs as fast as her feet can carry her, but it is too late. The rainbow shudders and lifts off high into the sky.

"Wait, please," Jessica cries, but the rainbow continues to climb, leaving her behind.

Jessica kicks the head off a dandelion in frustration before slumping to the ground sulking. As she sits pulling at the grass in disappointment, she hears a noise coming from the sky.

Looking up, she can hardly believe her eyes as she sees Lucy sliding off the end of the rainbow.

Her excitement soon turns to anguish when she hears Lucy's squeals of fear.

Jumping up quickly, Jessica holds her hands out, determined to catch Lucy as she falls faster and faster, tumbling through the air.

Too frightened to look in case she misses, Jessica squeezes her eyes tightly shut and hopes for the best.

Slowly, Jessica peeks through one eye and sees Lucy sitting safely in her hands.

With a cheeky grin across her face, Lucy gives Jessica a big, long lick on the end of her nose.

"What are you doing here?" Jessica asks, giggling at the tingling of her nose.

"A message came from the woodland fairy; she needs my help."

"But there is no woodland here."

"Of course, there is. You just can't see it. It's over there," Lucy says, turning around in Jessica's hand. "Come on, I'll show you."

With Lucy standing in her hands directing the way, Jessica sets off walking.

Suddenly, a powerful force begins to pull Jessica, sucking her through an invisible barrier.

A strange sensation turns her legs to jelly and she stumbles, dropping Lucy in the undergrowth.

Feeling fuzzy and more than a little confused, Jessica carefully begins to stand. Then, she jumps in shock as a high-pitched angry voice shouts out.

"Do you mind? Watch where you're standing."

Jessica looks around, trying to locate the owner of the voice.

"You can't see me because you're stood on me." The same voice calls out indignantly.

Jessica steps back, looking down at a flattened flower bristling itself back into shape.

"Oh," Jessica squeals, putting her hand to her mouth. "I'm so sorry, are you alright?"

"Apart from being stood on, perfectly," the flower responds snootily.

Remembering about Lucy, Jessica calls out to her.

Lucy's fluffy nose pops out from underneath the leaf of the flower. Jessica bends down to pick Lucy up, then quickly slips her into her pocket as she sees a group of mice running towards them shouting.

One mouse, with a shiny red waistcoat and matching bow tie, mumbles loudly as he scrambles up Jessica's dungarees.

"No, no, you can't be here. It's not right, not right at all."

Jessica walks backwards as the little mouse comes nose to nose with her.

"You're human," the mouse exclaims wide-eyed. "Humans can't be here; it will destroy everything. You must leave now."

The other mice push and pull at Jessica's legs, and she falls back into a tree.

"Go. Go now before any more damage is done," a squirrel warns, swinging from the tree by its tail.

"Go now," the tree booms, opening its cavern of a mouth, causing Jessica to almost fall inside.

Jessica covers her ears from the anger and shouting coming from every direction.

"Calm little ones. She is here to help, not harm," a gentle voice drifts through the air.

The little mouse gulps and crawls back down Jessica's dungarees. Head bowed, he backs away, straightening his bow tie.

Fluttering above them is a beautiful fairy. An emerald green dress delicately flows against her pale skin, shining like velvet, and the red of her hair shimmers in the light. Around her, lots of tiny fairies, like specks of light, flick and flutter.

"Please forgive my little friends; they are afraid. The barrier at the opposite end of the wood is breaking down. We have been invaded by a Dueno; our world is at its mercy. Our land is being destroyed and my magic alone cannot combat it."

The fairy lands delicately in front of Jessica. "This is why I sent a message for Lucy the unicorn. Is she here?"

Lucy pops her head out from Jessica's pocket and jumps out. The fairy's face falls.

"Oh dear, that won't do, it won't do at all,"

Lucy twitches her horn in confusion.

"You are even smaller than the mice; you will easily get lost." Waving her wand, she begins to chant a spell.

"This form is too small; increase
in size, strength and power.
On leaving this land,
reduce once more
to her tiny
form."

Lucy's body begins to tingle as she changes into a fully grown unicorn. Her body is now the colour of pearls with a white flowing mane, tinged pink at the tips.

"Please, we have little time; we must go," the woodland fairy urges, swiftly taking flight.

"Can I walk with you?" The mouse with the shiny red waistcoat asks shyly. Jessica smiles, scooping him up and placing him on Lucy's back.

"My name is Stanley," the little mouse says, holding his thin hand out.

"Well, I'm very pleased to meet you Stanley, my name is Jessica," she replies, taking his hand.

As they walk, Jessica takes in all the beauty around her: the sound of the birds, the sweet smell

of flowers, the buzzing of the bumble
bees and the fluttering of butterflies.

But as they continue to walk, the
colours seem to fade. Some trees still
stand, but their trunks are grey and
their branches dying. Others are already
reduced to grey dust. There is no sound
from the birds, no flowers, no life.

"My goodness, what
has happened? "

"It is the Dueno,"
Stanley says simply.

"Lucy, what is it; what's wrong?" Jessica asks anxiously, as Lucy cries out shaking her head.

"I can hear their cries, feel their pain. It fills my head, I cannot breathe. The trees and flowers are calling out for help."

"It's the Dueno's fault. We should find him," Stanley shouts, standing on Lucy's back then jumping down, gathering the other mice.

"No, please wait. You made a mistake when you thought I was here to harm you," Jessica pleads.

Lucy suddenly gives out a high pitched cry before crumpling to the ground. Jessica drops down next to her, stroking her face.

"The Dueno has put a curse on her; we must hunt him down," Stanley calls, jumping and swinging on a dead branch, breaking it off.

"Come on, let's go," he shouts, sending a rallying cry out as he runs off with the stick in his hand in search of the Dueno.

"You must go after them," Lucy manages to whisper. "Not Dueno's fault," she gasps, closing her eyes.

Jessica hugs Lucy tightly, tears rolling down her face. "I can't leave you," she sniffs.

The woodland fairy lands next to Jessica, resting her hand gently on her shoulder.

"I will take care of Lucy; now go quickly."

Kissing Lucy, Jessica runs after the woodland animals, but they are much faster than she is.

Using their sense of smell, the group of animals pick up the Dueno's scent.

"Look at these footprints," one of them calls out. Stanley rushes over to inspect the large flat footprints left in the grey dust.

"They're his, come on, this way," Stanley orders, following the trail which leads to a large toadstool, under which a den has been dug.

"Come on out Dueno, we know you are in there," Stanley demands.

From under the toadstool, a little face emerges. Long pointy ears stick out from a large floppy hat as he peers warily through a straggly fringe.

"You have put a curse on the unicorn and you are destroying our world," Stanley shouts.

"No, I know not of a unicorn," the Dueno sniffles.

"We don't believe you," Stanley stamps his scrawny little foot in temper. The Dueno scampers in fright, howling in fear.

Jessica follows the howling noise to find Stanley and his friends surrounding the pitiful looking creature.

"Leave him Stanley," Jessica calls out.

The mouse looks around as Jessica walks towards the cowering creature.

Crouched down, his large feet protrude from his dumpy little legs and rotund belly.

"Please, I will not hurt you," Jessica soothes the frightened creature. "Tell me what you want from this land?"

The Dueno looks at Jessica with caution.

"My world is grey; the colours and brightness attracted me," he explains. I didn't mean any harm; I just wanted to come and play. Then like me, everything turned grey. My fault. It's all my fault. I couldn't make it halt."

"None of this is your fault," Jessica reassures him.

The Dueno looks up hopefully through the peak of his hat.

"Please, can you help us? I promise no harm will come to you. My friend is sick and very weak. I think you can help her and help the woodland too. Please will you come?" Jessica asks gently, holding out her hand.

The small creature, with his big round cheeks and bulbous nose, reaches out his large spatula hand. Jessica takes him into her arms and runs.

"How is Lucy?" Jessica calls out to the fairy running to Lucy's side.

"She is weak. We must hurry."

The Dueno stares down at Lucy, then begins walking around her, mumbling.

"Let me take your pain so you will be well again."

Placing his hands over Lucy, he moves them rhythmically back and forth across her body. Slowly, Lucy opens her eyes. Jessica strokes her face, planting kisses on her nose.

"Patience child," the Dueno whispers. Concentrating harder now, beads of sweat drip from his forehead. Crouching over, he holds his round stomach in pain, as Lucy slowly begins to move and gradually gets back on her feet.

"Oh thank you, I don't know what I would do if I lost Lucy," Jessica says, hugging the little Dueno, then throwing her arms around Lucy's neck.

"Thank you," Lucy says simply. Bending down nuzzling the Dueno.

"We have one more favour to ask," the woodland fairy says. "Please help us close the barrier and save this land. It will come at a cost though, you will not be able to return to your world."

The Dueno stares hard at the ground then looks up awkwardly towards the mice. Stanley wrinkles his nose and steps forward.

"You have saved the unicorn; if you help save our land, you will be one of us and accepted into our world."

"Very well," the Dueno nods.

Lucy shakes rainbow dust from her horn, as the fairy waves her wand, sending the dust dancing and darting in all different directions.

Holding his hands in the air, the Dueno gathers the dust into a ball. Pulling his hands back, he then thrusts them forward.

The ball of dust crashes into the barrier, sending sparks of light this way and that, and then the barrier becomes invisible again.

"Look," Stanley shouts, jumping up and down in excitement. Everyone turns to stare.

The Dueno changes colour in front of their eyes. His large floppy hat is now as red as his big red cheeks and nose. A blue jacket complements a green waistcoat which matches the turn-ups of his yellow check trousers.

Across the woodland, colour begins to appear. Trees that were grey and fallen stand proud again, and everywhere flowers bloom and birds fly.

"Look at me!" the Dueno shouts, dancing a jig, revelling in his newfound colour. All his dreams have come true; he will never live in a grey world again.

"I told you, you would be one of us," Stanley laughs out loud. The two quickly forget their differences as Stanley joins the Dueno dancing his jig.

The dancing and singing last into the night until Lucy and Jessica have to go.

Jessica climbs onto Lucy's back and waves goodbye to their new friends.

Lucy canters through the woods, picking up speed to a gallop.

The moon shimmers and dances across Lucy's sleek body. The trees and flowers bend and sway their gratitude, creating a sweet song in the air.

Jumping through the barrier, Jessica lands hard on the ground as Lucy returns to her tiny form.

"Quick Lucy, look, the rainbow," Jessica shouts, picking Lucy up and running.

"See you soon Jessica," Lucy squeaks as she wraps her hooves around the rainbow.

"Hold on tight," Jessica says as the rainbow lifts off and soars high above the clouds.

Jessica watches as the rainbow and Lucy disappear. With one final wave and a contented smile, Jessica turns and walks back towards her grandmother's white stone cottage.

What is a Dueno?

In Spanish, Filipino and Portuguese folklore there is a word – *duende* – which literally means goblin, ghost or spirit. It is thought to have come from *"dueño de casa"*, meaning *"owner of a house".*

My idea for this book was to have a mischievous spirit that manages to enter the magic woodland. The fact that a *duende*, or *dueno*, is a spirit that can inhabit a dwelling fits perfectly with the story and helps explain why the woodland animals feel he is responsible for the destruction of their home.

Oh, and I thought the *dueno* sounded cute, so that was why I chose it for the character name.

SJ Dawson

Lightning Source UK Ltd.
Milton Keynes UK
UKHW050259110422
401355UK00002B/2